Pets on Parade

Don't miss a single

Nancy Drew
Clue Book:

Nancy Drew
* CLUE BOOK *
#6

Pets on Parade

BY CAROLYN KEENE * ILLUSTRATED BY PETER FRANCIS

Aladdin
NEW YORK   LONDON   TORONTO   SYDNEY   NEW DELHI

ALADDIN

An imprint of Simon & Schuster Children's Publishing Division
1230 Avenue of the Americas, New York, NY 10020
This Aladdin hardcover edition October 2016
Text copyright © 2016 by Simon & Schuster, Inc.
Illustrations copyright © 2016 by Peter Francis
Also available in an Aladdin paperback edition.
ALADDIN is a trademark of Simon & Schuster, Inc., and related logo
is a registered trademark of Simon & Schuster, Inc.
NANCY DREW, NANCY DREW CLUE BOOK, and colophons
are registered trademarks of Simon & Schuster, Inc.
All rights reserved, including the right of reproduction in whole or in part in any form.
For information about special discounts for bulk purchases, please contact
Simon & Schuster Special Sales at 1-866-506-1949 or business@simonandschuster.com.
The Simon & Schuster Speakers Bureau can bring authors to your live event.
For more information or to book an event contact the Simon & Schuster Speakers Bureau
at 1-866-248-3049 or visit our website at www.simonspeakers.com.
Designed by Karina Granda
The illustrations for this book were rendered digitally.
The text of this book was set in Adobe Garamond Pro.
Manufactured in the United States of America 0916 FFG
2 4 6 8 10 9 7 5 3 1
Library of Congress Control Number 2015043706
ISBN 978-1-4814-5824-5 (hc)
ISBN 978-1-4814-5823-8 (pbk)
ISBN 978-1-4814-5825-2 (eBook)

* CONTENTS *

Chapter

1

CHIP, CHIP, HOORAY!

"I don't get it, Nancy," eight-year-old George Fayne admitted. "If Chocolate Chip is dressed up as a vampire, then where are her fangs?"

Nancy Drew, also eight, couldn't answer. She was too busy trying to keep her puppy from chasing a squirrel in the park!

"Dogs already have pointy teeth, George," Bess Marvin, Nancy's other best friend said. "Like furry vampires."

"Chip howls like a vampire too." Nancy giggled

as the squirrel ran away. "But only when she sees a squirrel!"

"I thought only werewolves howl!" George said.

"Maybe vampire dogs do too!" Nancy joked.

It was Friday afternoon and a few days before Halloween. Thanks to Mayor Strong the Halloween fun had already begun in River Heights, starting with a Howl-a-ween Pet Parade on Saturday.

"Neat!" Bess said as the friends gazed around the park. "It's like all the pets in River Heights are here."

"But only *one* pet will get to lead the Howl-a-ween Parade," Nancy reminded her. "Hopefully the judges will like Chip in the pet show today and pick her!"

The judges were already seated at a picnic table. Instead of a picnic basket, lemonade, and potato salad, the table was covered with papers and pens.

"I know all the judges' names!" Bess said. "They're Ted and Tanya Rupert, the owners of the Fur-Ever Glam Pet Salon; Dr. Emily Poulos, a veterinarian; and Felipe Gomez!"

"Felipe Gomez?" Nancy exclaimed. "He's a dog-trainer superstar!"

Almost anyone with a dog knew Felipe and his web series *The Peaceful Pet*. Felipe trained dogs the Felipe Way. That day he would demonstrate his method on a River Heights dog—Mayor Strong's big drooling dog, Huey!

"The judges look like they're getting ready for the pet show soon," George pointed out. "Do you think Chip is ready, Nancy?"

Nancy nodded. She knew Chip would behave as the pets marched single-file past the judges' table. But good behavior wasn't the only thing the judges would look for.

"I hope Felipe and the other judges like Chip's vampire costume best," Nancy said. "It once belonged to Murray the Monster Mutt!"

"Who?" Bess asked.

Nancy pointed to the three *M*'s stitched to the back of the cape. "Murray the Monster Mutt had his own TV show before we were born. My dad found Murray's cape at a vintage clothes store on Main Street!"

"I heard about that show from my mom and dad," George said. "But where's Murray now?"

"I don't have a clue," Nancy admitted. "I just know that Murray lived right here in River Heights—"

"And now he's a ghost-dog!" someone cut in.

Nancy turned to see Quincy Taylor from the girls' third grade class. Perched on Quincy's shoulder was his ferret, Slinky, dressed as a clown.

"What do you mean? What's a ghost-dog?" Nancy asked.

"Dogs don't live as long as humans do," Quincy explained. "So Murray has got to be a ghost by now."

"Not if Murray really *is* a vampire dog," George informed. "Then he'd live forever!"

Quincy pointed to Chip's cape. "Aren't you scared that Murray's cape will turn your dog into a Monster Mutt too?"

"No way!" Nancy chuckled. "I've heard of haunted houses, not haunted capes!"

"And we're detectives," Bess pointed out proudly. "So if there were ghosts around, we'd have found them by now!"

Nancy nodded in agreement. She, Bess, and George loved solving mysteries more than anything. So much that they started their own detective club called the Clue Crew. Nancy even had a Clue Book where she wrote down every suspect and clue!

"Whatever." Quincy sighed as he handed a small white card to Nancy. "But if your dog acts weird give us a call."

As Quincy walked away the girls checked out his card.

"'Ghost Grabbers Club,'" Nancy read out loud. "'We catch ghosts so you don't have to.'"

"Put it away, Nancy," Bess insisted. "Quincy's ghost club sounds superscary."

"Speaking of scary," George said in a low voice. "Look who else is here."

Nancy looked up from Quincy's card to see

Deirdre Shannon walking toward them. Prancing in front of her was her fluffy new bichon frise.

"The dog's name is Princess Pom-Pom," Nancy whispered.

"How do you know?" Bess whispered too.

"Deirdre wrote about Pom-Pom in her blog, *Dishing with Deirdre*," Nancy explained.

George rolled her eyes. Deirdre Shannon usually got whatever she wanted—like her own blog and now a puppy.

"If Pom-Pom is a princess, that makes Deirdre a queen," George said. "A *drama* queen!"

Deirdre stopped in front of the girls. She beamed proudly at Princess Pom-Pom, dressed like a real princess with a sparkly doggy gown and headdress.

"Pom-Pom looks cute today, Deirdre." Nancy smiled.

"*Princess* Pom-Pom!" Deirdre corrected. "She just had a mani-pedi at Fur-Ever Glam Pet Salon. And a wash and blowout."

"I think they blew a little too hard," George joked.

"Very funny," Deirdre snapped. "I'll bet you didn't know Princess Pom-Pom also has her own lady-in-waiting."

As if on cue, Sage Tenowitz from the second grade rushed over. Water splashed from a crystal dish she carried.

"I was just getting Princess Pom-Pom's vitamin water, Deirdre," Sage said, placing the dish down on the ground. "Should I give Pom-Pom her foot massage after that?"

"You touch doggy feet?" Bess wrinkled her nose.

While Deirdre leaned down to Pom-Pom, Sage whispered to the girls, "I'll do anything for Pom-Pom. Deirdre promised I could hang out with her and her cool friends for a whole week if I did!"

"Was that a promise or a threat?" George teased.

"Heard that, Georgia Fayne!" Deirdre sneered.

George cringed at the sound of Georgia, her real name. She hated it more than broccoli-flavored jelly beans!

"Do you have a dog too, Sage?" Bess asked.

"No," Sage admitted. "But I have lots of stuffed animals, and one looks just like Pom-Pom."

Deirdre leaned in toward Nancy, Bess, and George and said, "Who needs stuffed when you can have the real deal?"

Suddenly—*"Wooooooo!"*

Chip began howling as she strained on her leash. Another gray squirrel with a bushy tail scurried by!

"Will you make Chip stop, Nancy?" Deirdre demanded as she scooped up Pom-Pom. "She's scaring the princess!"

"She'll stop when the squirrel runs away," Nancy explained. "Chip only goes nuts when she sees squirrels."

"Nuts, squirrels." George laughed. "Good one, Nancy!"

Deirdre tossed her hair and then huffed off with Pom-Pom. Picking up the doggy dish, Sage hurried after.

"Deirdre may be snooty," Nancy admitted, "but Princess Pom-Pom is kind of cute."

"I wish I had a fluffy little dog like Pom-Pom," Bess said. "What kind of a dog do you want, George?"

"Hmm . . . probably a robotic dog," George remarked.

"Surprise, surprise." Nancy giggled.

Bess and George were cousins but as different as a Chihuahua and a bulldog. Bess loved girly girl clothes and accessories for her long blond hair. Dark-haired George only cared about how comfortable her clothes were. And her favorite accessories were electronic gadgets!

"Okay!" Nancy declared as she tugged Chip's leash. "Let's get this Monster Mutt away from that poor squirrel."

Nancy, Bess, and George strolled with Chip through the park decorated for the pet contest. There were orange balloons tied to trees and painted pumpkins everywhere!

Also there were more kids from school. Andrea Wu was walking her lively terrier, Angus, who was dressed like a superhero. Kevin Garcia's beagle, Hudson, looked funny as a dragon. Shelby Metcalf's new parrot, Ernie, made the perfect pirate with a buccaneer's hat and silver medallion around his feathery neck.

"Look!" Bess pointed out. "Felipe Gomez started his dog-training demonstration!"

"Let's watch!" Nancy said.

Nancy, Bess, and George rushed to join a small crowd watching Felipe train Huey. The mayor's big dog obeyed the sit and beg commands perfectly. But then—

"Woof!" Huey barked as he leaped up on Felipe. Resting huge paws on Felipe's shoulders, Huey licked Felipe's face with a loud *SLUURRRRRRP!*

Everyone laughed as an embarrassed Felipe

turned to the crowd.
"H-Huey is saying
th-thank-you—thank
you for teaching me
the Felipe Way!"

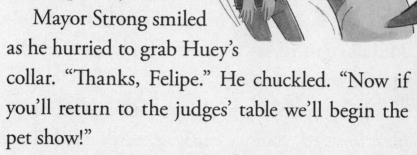

Mayor Strong smiled
as he hurried to grab Huey's
collar. "Thanks, Felipe." He chuckled. "Now if
you'll return to the judges' table we'll begin the
pet show!"

"This is it!" Nancy said excitedly.

Nancy and Chip fell in line with the other kids
and their pets. As they began to march, Nancy
heard barks, meows, and squawks, but not from
Chip. Her puppy's tail wagged cheerily as they
strutted calmly past the judges.

"Good girl, Chip," Nancy told her dog.

But just as the last pet, a cat dressed as a candy
corn, walked past the judges' table—

"*Eeek!* That boy has a *skunk*!"

"Skunk?" Nancy gasped.

The crowd spread out as Antonio Elefano

walked forward carrying a cage. Sure enough there was a skunk inside!

Everyone in the girls' class knew Antonio was a jokester, but nobody knew he had a skunk—until now!

"I got Romeo just in time for Halloween"—Antonio grinned—"and he's ready to lead the Howl-a-ween Parade!"

"Sorry, young man," Mayor Strong said, stepping forward, "but we can't have a wild skunk in the parade. What if he sprayed his stinky stuff?"

"Romeo's not wild." Antonio placed the cage on the floor and pulled up the door. "He's totally tame. See?"

Romeo seemed to yawn as he padded out from the cage. He sniffed the air before heading in Chip's direction!

"No, no, *no!*" Nancy cried.

Using both of her hands, Nancy pulled Chip away from Romeo, but it was too late. The skittish skunk turned, lifted his tail, and—*PFFFFFFT*—*sprayed!*

Chapter

2

WHAT STINKS?

Nancy was too shocked to scream. Chip's Murray the Monster Mutt cape was soaked!

"That dog smells funky!" a girl cried out.

"You mean skunky!" shouted another boy, laughing.

Chip seemed stunned, but she didn't make a fuss—even when everybody else did.

In a flash Nancy was joined by her friends.

Bess pointed her finger at Antonio. "It's all your fault, Antonio Elefano!"

"Yeah!" George agreed. "Whoever heard of a pet skunk?"

"Take that skunk away now, please," Mayor Strong insisted as Antonio hustled Romeo back into his cage.

"Okay." Antonio sighed as he carried the cage away. "But what's a skunk supposed to smell like—roses?"

Bess put a gentle hand on Nancy's shoulder. "Chip will be okay, Nancy."

"Sure, she will," George agreed. "It's just her cape that smells like a science experiment gone bad!"

"But now Chip can't compete in the costume contest." Nancy sighed. "I guess she won't be able to lead the Howl-a-ween Parade this year."

"Not so!" someone piped up.

Who said that? Nancy looked up to see three of the judges.

"Your dog stayed calm through the whole ordeal," Dr. Poulos remarked. "That's the kind of pet I'd like to see leading the parade!"

"So would I," Tanya Rupert agreed. "Especially

dressed like Murray the Monster Mutt!"

"Murray the Monster Mutt used to be our favorite show," Ted Rupert said. "Chip should lead the parade!"

"Omigosh!" Nancy exclaimed with surprise.

"Besides," Dr. Poulos went on, "Tanya, Ted, and I already picked Chip based on her excellent behavior during the show."

"That's right," Ted agreed. "The pet who came in second place was that princess pup."

An angry yelp arose from the crowd. Nancy was sure it was Deirdre's!

"Thank you very much!" Nancy said. "But what about the skunky smell?"

"Just soak the cape in tomato juice," Dr. Poulos advised. "That should get the smell out."

Nancy flashed a relieved smile. Not only was Chip still in the contest—she had just won!

"Thank you, again!" Nancy told the judges happily. But not everyone was happy.

"Wait a minute!" Deirdre demanded as she pushed through the crowd. Sage followed her with Pom-Pom. "Princess Pom-Pom smells like strawberry doggy shampoo—not skunk!"

"So what's your point?" Ted asked.

"Sooooo," Deirdre said in a singsongy voice. "Princess Pom-Pom should be leading the parade, not Chip."

Then Felipe stormed over with Huey's leash clutched in his fist. "Huey is a natural to lead the Howl-a-ween Parade! He was trained the Felipe Way!"

Then Huey piddled on Felipe's leg. George could barely keep it together. Felipe didn't notice as he turned to Mayor Strong and asked, "What do you say, Your Honor?"

Mayor Strong shrugged his shoulders and said, "Of course I was hoping Huey would lead the parade. . . ."

Nancy's heart dropped. Until—

"But three out of four judges chose Chip," Mayor Strong added with a smile. "Since majority rules, Chocolate Chip will lead the parade!"

"Yes!" Nancy cheered under her breath.

After trading high fives with Bess and George, Nancy smiled at her dog. "Hear that, girl? You're leading the Howl-a-ween Parade!"

She looked up to see the other kids holding their noses. "Um . . . after we wash your cape!"

"Do you think tomato juice is enough?" Bess asked.

"Dr. Poulos seemed to think so," Nancy replied.

The three friends stared down at Chip's cape soaking in the juice-filled basin on the laundry-room counter.

Hannah Gruen, the Drews' housekeeper, picked up the empty juice bottle for recycling. "You girls are lucky I bought a bottle of tomato juice at the

supermarket today," Hannah told them with a smile.

"Thanks, Hannah," Nancy said, smiling too. "It's as if you read my mind!"

Hannah gave her a wink before leaving the room. She didn't read minds, but she did know Nancy inside and out. That's because Hannah had known her since Nancy was three years old. She was also like a mother to Nancy, reminding her to wear her rain boots, do her homework, and eat all her string beans!

"Once, my mom got stinky fish oil on her blouse at a catering job," George explained. "She soaked her blouse in lemon juice and vinegar, and it got the fishy smell out!"

Lemon juice and vinegar? Nancy's eyes lit up. She would try anything to make sure the skunky smell came out.

"Let's try that too!" Nancy declared.

"Tomato juice, lemon, and vinegar?" Bess chuckled. "Are we soaking a stinky cape or making spaghetti sauce?"

"Who cares as long as it works!" George stated.

"It's got to work!" Nancy called on her way to the kitchen. "The parade is tomorrow and Chip will be ready!"

The next morning Nancy, Bess, and George headed to Main Street and the Howl-a-ween Pet Parade. With them was Chip wearing the Murray the Monster Mutt vest but not the cape. That was draped carefully over Nancy's arm.

"Wowee!" Bess exclaimed as they turned onto Main Street. "Look how many people came to watch the parade!"

"And the parade leader Chip!" Nancy added proudly. She was happy to see other costumed pets and their owners—except one . . .

Deirdre stormed over with Princess Pom-Pom. "No way could you have gotten that gross stink out of Chip's cape!"

"After washing it in a few secret ingredients," Bess explained, "Chip's vampire cape smells fresh as a daisy."

"Take a whiff!" George suggested.

"No, thank you." Deirdre huffed. She nodded at the cape over Nancy's arm. "If the cape is clean, why isn't Chip wearing it?"

"I'll tie it on when she's up on the hay wagon," Nancy answered. "Just in case Antonio shows up with Romeo again."

"Where's Sage, Deirdre?" George asked. "Shouldn't she be here to help Pom-Pom before she marches in the parade?"

"That's *Princess* Pom-Pom to you," Deirdre corrected, "And Sage had something else to do."

Deirdre hugged Pom-Pom close. She then turned on her heel and huffed off.

"I guess Princess Pom-Pom's lady-in-waiting decided not to wait!" Bess giggled.

"Well, I can't wait for this parade!" Nancy stated. "Let's check out the hay wagon we'll get to ride!"

The usually bustling Main Street was closed to traffic for the parade. The girls walked up the middle of the street until they spotted the hay wagon. It was painted bright red and hitched to a shiny black car.

"Cool!" Nancy exclaimed, gazing up at the wagon. It was filled to the top with yellow pieces of hay. Also in the wagon were a few small bales.

"It smells just like a farm!" Bess said, taking a long whiff. "A farm in the fall!"

"That's because it is from a farm." George pointed to the words CRUNCH APPLE FARMS painted on one side. "See?"

"I went apple-picking at Crunch Apple Farms with my dad last year!" Nancy said. "We picked McIntosh, Golden Delicious—"

"*Raaaak!*" something squawked.

Nancy, Bess, and George looked up in time to see a parrot flutter toward the wagon. The parrot was dressed as a pirate for the parade. It hovered over the wagon before gently landing on a bale of hay.

"That's Shelby's parrot, Ernie," Nancy recognized.

"But where's Shelby?" Bess asked.

"Maybe she's on the other side of the wagon," George decided. "Let's check it out."

The girls walked around the wagon but stopped short when they saw Felipe Gomez. The celebrity dog trainer stood next to the wagon, blinking nervously while digging into his pocket.

"What's he doing?" Nancy whispered.

Before they could find out, a woman wearing a headset and holding a clipboard walked over. "I'm Kim Adamo, the parade director," Kim introduced herself. She smiled down at Chip. "Is that the dog who's leading the parade?"

"This is Chip!" Nancy confirmed proudly. "I'll tie her vampire cape on as soon as we get up on the wagon."

"The time is now," Kim said. "The parade has to kick off in ten minutes sharp!"

"On it!" Nancy promised.

The girls hurried with Chip toward to the hay wagon. Felipe was gone, and Ernie had flown onto Shelby's shoulder.

"Good luck, you guys!" Shelby called.

"Good luck, good luck!" Ernie repeated. *"Arrrrk!"*

After being helped up on the wagon, the girls settled on the hay with Chip. George immediately pulled a computer tablet from her backpack.

"What are you doing?" Bess asked as George held the tablet facing the crowds on Main Street.

"Parade cam!" George explained. "I'm going to film the parade so we don't miss a beat!"

Nancy slipped Chip's leash into her messenger

bag and then tied the Murray the Monster Cape around Chip's neck.

"Who's the best parade leader ever?" Nancy asked.

Chip cocked her head happily and wagged her tail.

The girls glanced back at the other march-ers. One was Deirdre walking Pom-Pom on a rhinestone-studded leash. Deirdre's eyes narrowed as she glared up at Nancy, Bess, and George.

"Oh, get over it!" George muttered, still hold-ing the tablet facing the crowds.

Nancy was about to adjust Chip's cape when—

"Woof, woof, whine, whine!"

Nancy stared at Chip and gasped. Her puppy wasn't just barking and whining. She was rolling over and over from her tummy to her back, four legs kicking in the air!

"Woof, woof!" Roll, kick. *"Whine, whine!"* Roll, kick. *"Woof!"* Roll. *"Whine!"* Kick. *"Wooooooooo!!!"*

"Chip!" Nancy cried over the earsplitting howl. "What's the matter?"

In a flash, Kim climbed aboard. "What on earth is wrong with your dog?"

"I don't know, Ms. Adamo," Nancy admitted. "Chip was great a few minutes ago!"

"Well, now she's doing the same thing over and over again," Kim observed. "And loudly!"

"*Woof, woof!*" Roll, kick. "*Whine, whine!*" Roll, kick. "*Woof!*" Roll. "*Whine!*" Kick. "*Woooooooo!!!*"

"We cannot have a crazy dog leading the parade," Kim insisted. "I'm afraid Chip will have to be replaced."

Nancy, Bess, and George traded horrified looks. Did they just hear what they thought they heard?

Chapter

3

SQUAWK TALK

"Hurry, girls, please," Kim called. "We have to replace Chocolate Chip right now and begin the parade!"

By now Chip was rolling so fast her cape came undone, sliding out from under her.

Nancy's heart ached as they were helped down from the hay wagon. Chip's hind foot dragged the cape as she jumped down after them. As the cape fluttered to the ground, George grabbed it and stuffed it inside her backpack next to her tablet.

Nancy hoped Chip still had a chance. "Can't you please give Chip a do-over, Ms. Adamo?" she asked. "Look at how calm she is now."

Chip was covered with hay but mellow as she panted cheerily.

"I'm sorry, but what if Chip acts up again?" Kim explained. She began looking around at the other kids and their pets. "We'll have to go with the pet that came in second place."

Deirdre pushed her way through the crowd with Pom-Pom. "*That* would be Princess Pom-Pom!" she declared.

Kim looked at Pom-Pom and nodded. "She was the runner-up. The princess pup will lead the parade."

"Awesome!" Deirdre exclaimed and then under her breath sneered, "It worked."

Nancy, Bess, and George traded puzzled looks. What worked?

"The parade will start in exactly three minutes!" Kim shouted out. "Owners and pets line up behind the wagon!"

Deirdre climbed up on the wagon, sitting on a hay bale as if it were a throne. Holding Pom-Pom on her lap, Deirdre smiled at the girls. It wasn't a very nice smile either. Nancy frowned to herself. How did this happen? What made Chip suddenly go bonkers?

"Nancy," Bess said softly, "Chip may not be able to lead the parade, but maybe she can still march in it."

"That could be fun." George shrugged. "Kind of."

Nancy shook her head as she brushed pieces of hay from Chip's chocolate-brown fur. How could she have fun after what just happened? She had important work to do!

"No parade for me or Chip," Nancy replied as she hooked on Chip's leash. "I need to find out why Chip went nutters the way she did."

"I had a feeling you'd say that!" George grinned.

"So did I," Bess agreed. "This is definitely a case for the Clue Crew!"

But just as the Clue Crew and Chip were about to squeeze through the crowd—

"Nancy, Bess, George!" a boy called. "Wait up!"

Nancy turned to see Quincy Taylor and his friends.

"We saw Chip acting like a dog possessed," Quincy said, "Which is why you need—"

"The Ghost Grabbers!" his friends chorused.

Nancy rolled her eyes. Not that silly club again!

"Did you ever wonder if the ghost of Murray the Monster Mutt wants his old cape back?" Quincy asked with wide eyes. "And he won't leave Chip alone until he gets it?"

"Why don't you guys act like ghosts?" George snapped. "And disappear!"

"You may not need us now," Quincy said, "but when you change your minds, you know where to find us!"

Not looking back, the girls headed to a less-crowded part of Main Street. There they found a pet-friendly place called Lisa's Bowwow Meow-Meow Café. Since most pets were at the parade, Chip was the only dog there.

While Chip chewed a biscuit shaped like a sneaker, the girls sat around a table. They waited for their hot apple ciders to cool, and Nancy pulled out her Clue Book.

"You really do carry your Clue Book everywhere, Nancy," Bess noted. "Even to parades!"

Nancy tapped her chin thoughtfully with the cupcake-shaped eraser on her favorite pencil. Her eyes lit up after the fourth tap.

"I'm going to call this case, 'What Made Chip Flip?'" Nancy decided. She wrote the words at the top of a clean page. Skipping a few lines she wrote the word *Suspects*.

"Who would have done something to upset Chip?" Bess wondered. "That's what I want to know!"

"I think Deirdre Shannon is suspect number one," George said. "She was mad that the judges picked Chip instead of Pom-Pom."

"And when Pom-Pom was picked, Deirdre said, 'It worked,'" Nancy pointed out. "As if she had a secret plan!"

"But how could Deirdre make Chip flip?" Bess asked.

"I don't know," Nancy admitted as she wrote Deirdre's name in her Clue Book. "But I do know that Deirdre Shannon is suspect number one—"

"Numero uno! Numero uno!" something squawked. *"Raaaak!"*

The girls looked up to see a parrot zoom through an open window into the café. A parrot dressed as a pirate!

"It's Ernie!" Nancy declared as Shelby's pet parrot fluttered over their heads toward the counter. Lisa stepped out from behind her counter, hands on her hips.

"We don't serve unattended pets in here," Lisa called out. "Whose parrot is this?"

Then the door swung open and Shelby ran inside.

"There's Ernie!" Shelby sighed with relief. "When the parade marched by the café, all he could think about was bird food!"

"Chow time, chow time!" Ernie squawked. *"Raaaaak!"* Ernie touched down on the counter. He grabbed a bird-seed churro, pecking it hungrily.

"Hey!" Lisa exclaimed.

"Hay!" Ernie repeated. "In the hay, in the hay! *Raaaaak!"*

Nancy blinked. "Did he just say . . . 'in the hay'?"

"Ernie must have heard that somewhere," Shelby explained. "Parrots always repeat what they hear."

While Shelby paid for the churro, Nancy, Bess, and George went back to sipping their apple cider.

"Lots of people say 'hey,'" Bess pointed out. "Ernie could have heard it anywhere."

"That's for sure." George nodded. "Remember when we found him on the hay wagon? That parrot gets around."

Hay wagon! Nancy's eyes lit up above the rim of her cider cup. Ernie was on the wagon. So was Felipe, creeping around and looking nervous!

"Unless Ernie repeated a different kind of hey," Nancy said slowly. "H-A-Y!"

Chapter 4

CLUE AT THE ZOO

"H-A-Y spells hay," Bess said excitedly. "As in hay wagon!"

"Ernie was on the wagon when Felipe was there too," Nancy explained. "What if Ernie saw Felipe hide something underneath the hay to upset Chip?"

"Felipe did want Huey to lead the parade, not Chip," Bess added.

"Ernie said, 'in the hay,'" George remembered. "Maybe that's what he heard Felipe say."

"Who would he say it to?" Nancy wondered. "Felipe was standing at the wagon alone."

"Some people talk to themselves," George said.

"And you talk in your sleep, George," Bess teased. "I heard you at a sleepover once. Blah, blah, blah—"

"And you snore like a dragon!" George snapped. "With a stuffy nose!"

Nancy formed the letter T with her hands as if to say time-out! "You guys—can we please talk about the case?"

"Okay, okay," George agreed. "What do we do next?"

"I want to check out the hay wagon," Nancy explained. "It will probably go back to Crunch Apple Farms after the parade."

"Then we should go there too!" Bess said excitedly. "I heard they have a petting zoo."

Ernie soared above the girls, squawking and spitting birdseed all over. "In the hay! In the hay! *Raaaak!*"

"Say it; don't spray it!" Nancy laughed. "But thanks for the great clue, Ernie!"

After bringing Chip home, the girls got a ride from Mr. Drew to Crunch Apple Farms. He planned to buy freshly baked pies while the girls looked for clues.

"Make sure you get permission to go near the wagon," Mr. Drew advised the girls when they reached the farm.

Nancy smiled. Her dad was a lawyer, so he loved to give advice. Lucky for her, most of it was great!

"We will, Daddy," Nancy promised. "And you make sure to get some cherry pies."

"You got it!" Mr. Drew chuckled.

After filing out of the car, the three friends made their way through Crunch Apple Farms, their feet rustling through colorful fallen leaves.

The farm was filled with bright-orange pumpkin stands, not-so-scary scarecrows, and barrels of red and green apples to buy. But where was the hay wagon?

"You guys, look!" Bess gasped.

"Is it the hay wagon?" Nancy asked.

"Almost as good," Bess said excitedly. "It's the petting zoo!"

Nancy and George followed Bess through a gate that opened onto a fenced-in pen. The pen was filled with baby goats and lambs!

"Bess, we can't play with the animals now!" Nancy called as Bess ran straight to a snowy white goat. "We have to look for the hay wagon!"

"You mean that one?" George asked.

Nancy followed George's gaze. Toward the back of the animal pen was a barn. Through the open door, Nancy spotted a red painted wagon. Was it the same wagon from the parade? There was one way to find out. . . .

"We're going in there," Nancy declared.

"What about the baby animals?" Bess asked as a baby goat licked her fingers.

"There's only one animal on my mind now," Nancy admitted. "And that's Chip!"

There were no other guests in the petting zoo

or inside the barn. Only haystacks, an overhead loft filled with more hay—and the wagon.

"How do we know it's the same wagon from the parade?" Bess asked.

"It's got Crunch Apple Farms painted on the side," George said. She stood on tiptoes to sniff the hay. "Plus it smells like strawberry doggy shampoo, so we know Pom-Pom was on it."

"*Princess* Pom-Pom!" Bess teased.

"Let's search the hay in the wagon before someone comes," Nancy said. "We never got permission to be in here."

"On it!" George declared. She climbed one of the wheels and jumped into the hay with a *PLOOF*. Quickly, George crawled to the spot where Felipe had been standing. She used her hands to dig through the loose hay until her eyes flashed.

"What is it, George?" Nancy asked.

George smiled as she pulled an orange-colored necktie out from under the hay. Jumping down from the wagon, George showed it to Nancy and Bess.

"That tie is ripped at the bottom," Nancy observed. "And there's a big blotchy stain on it."

"Gross!" Bess remarked.

"So is the goat spit on your fingers, Bess," George groaned.

Nancy studied the tie closely. "I don't remember Felipe wearing an orange tie before the parade. But I do remember him digging into his pocket."

"Maybe Felipe had that tie in his pocket," George thought out loud. "Maybe that's what he hid under the hay!"

Nancy shook her head. "That wouldn't make Chip flip. Not a plain old tie!"

"Maybe Felipe hid something else," Bess suggested. "Go back up there, George!"

George was about to climb up on the wagon when—*CREEEEEEAKKK!!!*

The girls glanced out the barn door. Outside was a man opening the petting zoo gate. His back was turned toward the barn as he stepped inside, closing the gate behind him.

"Who's that?" Bess whispered.

"Whoever it is he can't see us snooping here without permission," Nancy answered. "We have to hide!"

George stuffed the tie into her pocket. The girls found a tall haystack and darted behind it. After a few seconds, they quietly popped their heads above the hay.

Nancy, Bess, and George secretly watched. The man stood directly outside the barn door, looking right and then left.

When Nancy saw who he was, she whispered, "Bess, George—it's Felipe!"

Chapter

5

BYE-BYE TIE

Nancy, Bess, and George held their breaths as they watched Felipe from behind the haystack.

"Oh no!" Bess whispered. "What do we do if Felipe finds us with his tie?"

"We question him!" Nancy replied sternly.

Felipe headed straight to the hay wagon and to the spot where the tie was found. He dug his hand into the loose hay, and then he said, "This is exactly where I put it. Where is it?"

George turned to Nancy and Bess. "Felipe does talk to himself. I knew it!"

"And he's looking for his tie!" Nancy whispered.

The girls watched Felipe frantically dig through the hay, pieces flying. Suddenly, Nancy felt a tug on her shirt. Then—*"Baaaa!"*

Nancy gasped. It was one of the baby goats from the petting zoo! She looked to see if Felipe heard. Luckily, he was busily digging through the hay.

"Go back to the petting zoo," George hissed to the goat. "We're working here!"

The goat responded by playfully tugging George's sneaker lace.

Bess giggled—until the goat went from George's sneaker to Bess's jacket!

"Noooo!" Bess cried. "He's chewing my new suede-trimmed hoodie!"

"Baaaaa!" the goat bleated loudly.

This time Felipe looked up, staring at the haystack. The girls ducked, but it was too late.

"I saw you!" Felipe called. "Who's there?"

"Looks like he's got our goat," George muttered.

The goat bleated again before scurrying out of the barn. The girls slowly walked out from behind the haystack.

"Hi," Nancy said, forcing a smile.

"I know you!" Felipe remarked. "Didn't your dog lead the parade until she went crazy?"

"Chip is not crazy!" Nancy insisted. "We think something in the hay wagon made her act that way."

"Something like this!" George said, holding up

the ripped and blotched necktie. "Look familiar?"

Felipe's jaw dropped when he saw the tie. He then stuck out his palm and said, "I'll take that, please."

"So you were looking for this tie," George confirmed. "Which means you probably hid it in the hay too!"

"Oh, Huey!" Felipe murmured to himself.

Nancy blinked. "Did you just say 'Huey'?"

"As in Mayor Strong's dog?" Bess asked.

Felipe's throat bobbed as he gulped. "Absolutely not!" he blurted. "I said 'oh . . . phooey'!"

"I know a *phooey* from a *Huey*," George muttered. "Nice try, Felipe."

Nancy wondered why Felipe would mention the mayor's dog. Then something about the tie clicked.

"That rip looks like something a dog would make," Nancy pointed out. "And the blotch looks like dog slobber."

"And nobody slobbers like Huey slobbers," Bess added.

"Not true!" Felipe declared. "Huey was trained the Felipe Way. He passed Drool School with flying colors!"

"He didn't seem trained yesterday," Bess said. "We saw him jump on you. And piddle on your—"

"Stoppp!" Felipe cut in. "All right, it's true. Right before the Howl-a-ween Parade, Huey jumped on me again, ripping up and drooling all over my tie!"

"Huey was just being a dog," Nancy said.

"I know, I know." Felipe sighed. "But Mayor Strong wanted me to train Huey the Felipe Way. I couldn't let him see Huey fail!"

"So you hid the tie underneath the hay before the parade," George figured. "Did you hide anything else that would upset Chip?"

"Why would I do that?" Felipe asked.

"Maybe you wanted to spoil Chip's big moment," Nancy suggested, "because you wanted Huey to lead the parade."

"I did nothing of the kind," Felipe insisted. "Your puppy won the contest fair and square. Chip ruled . . . Huey drooled."

Nancy turned to Bess and George. "I don't think the tie made Chip nutters. Even if she smelled Huey's scent, she's great with other dogs."

"You're not going to show the tie to Mayor Strong," Felipe piped up, "are you?"

"We won't, but you should," George replied as she returned the tie to Felipe.

"Honesty should be the Felipe Way too!" Bess added.

Felipe paced back and forth, considering what Nancy suggested. He then stopped, smiled, and said, "Thank you, girls. I will tell Mayor Strong that Huey needs a bit more tutoring."

He pointed out the door to the petting zoo and said, "But first I'm going to train those goats the Felipe Way!"

Nancy, Bess, and George left the barn. As they filed out of the petting zoo gate Felipe was already training a baby lamb to sit!

"Our only other suspect is Deirdre Shannon," Nancy said, crossing Felipe's name off the suspect list. "But what could Deirdre have done to Chip?"

Still thinking, Nancy, Bess, and George walked through the farm. They stopped to sit on a haystack to think more and listen to a fiddler dressed as scarecrow. The fiddler-scarecrow was in the middle of playing "Turkey in the Straw" for an audience of kids.

"That straw man is awesome," George said, pulling out her tablet. "I'm going to film him."

"Wait, George," Bess said. "First show me what you filmed at the parade this morning."

"It couldn't be much." Nancy sighed. "We weren't there very long."

George turned off the sound so it wouldn't bother the fiddler. She then played the video from the parade. Nancy and Bess peered over George's shoulders to watch.

Nancy smiled

at the screen. It showed kids and grown-ups lined up along Main Street. Their faces were eagerly turned toward the Howl-a-ween Pet Parade. Some wore their Halloween costumes.

"If only Chip could have led the parade." Nancy sighed. "It would have been so much fun."

As the girls watched, some kind of stick jutted out of the crowd only a few feet away from the wagon. It was a pink fishing pole—with something hanging from it!

"What is that?" George asked.

"It looks like a stuffed animal swinging back and forth," Bess observed. "A stuffed animal with a bushy tail."

"A squirrel?" Nancy guessed. She wrinkled her brow in confusion. "What does a squirrel have to do with Halloween?"

"Maybe it was a silly joke," Bess said. "You can film the fiddler now, George—"

"Wait!" Nancy interrupted.

"Now what?" George asked.

Nancy stared at the tablet and the stuffed squirrel. "Maybe it wasn't a joke. Maybe it was meant to upset Chip!"

Chapter

6

SQUIRRELED AWAY

"Chip does bark at squirrels," Bess agreed. "Especially when they run up trees."

"Who would know that besides us?" George asked.

"Deirdre Shannon," Nancy replied. "She saw Chip bark at a squirrel in the park yesterday."

George's eyes flashed as she remembered. "Deirdre wanted Princess Pom-Pom to lead the parade instead of Chip," she said. "She could have used that squirrel to make Chip go bonkers!"

"But Deirdre was behind the hay wagon before the parade," Bess pointed out. "How could she be there and in the crowd at the same time?"

"Unless Deirdre got someone else to do it," Nancy said. "Like Princess Pom-Pom's lady-in-waiting!"

"Sage Tenowitz!" George shouted.

The scarecrow looked up from his fiddle at the outburst.

"Um, sorry!" George said quickly. "We were just going."

The Clue Crew left to find Mr. Drew. On the way, Nancy wrote Sage's name next to Deirdre's name in her Clue Book. Next to Sage's name she doodled a little squirrel.

"I just thought of something," George said as she watched Nancy draw the squirrel. "Didn't Sage say she had a lot of stuffed animals?"

"Yes!" Bess remembered. "Maybe one of those stuffed animals is a squirrel!"

"We should go to Sage's house to look for a

stuffed squirrel and a pink fishing pole," Nancy suggested.

George pointed to her tablet. "I'll e-mail my mom and ask her where Sage lives. She once catered a bridal shower at the Tenowitz house."

"Should we ask your dad to drive us to Sage's house right away, Nancy?" Bess asked.

Nancy waved to her dad in the distance. He was waiting for them near a stand that sold cakes, pies, and doughnuts.

"Not right away." Nancy smiled. "Even detectives need a break once and awhile. A doughnut break!"

"Are you sure this is the house, George?" Nancy asked after ringing the bell of a shiny yellow door.

The girls waited on a porch decorated with pumpkin-shaped lanterns for Halloween.

"My mom said this is the place." George shrugged. "Fifty-two Cornflower Road."

"I hope someone opens the door soon!" Bess complained. "This thing must weigh a ton!"

Bess shifted a painted pumpkin from one arm to the other. They had bought the pumpkin on their way out of Crunch Apple Farms for Sage.

Nancy reached out to ring again when the door swung open.

"Hello!" a woman greeted with a smile. "You must be Sage's friends. I'm her mom."

"We know Sage from school," Nancy explained politely. "Is she home?"

"Or," George said, raising an eyebrow, "is she out . . . fishing?"

"Not today," Mrs. Tenowitz said. "Sage is on her way home from tap-dance class. She's going fishing with her brother tomorrow."

"Score!" George whispered.

"We'd like to give Sage a pumpkin we got at the farm," Nancy told Mrs. Tenowitz. "Since we can't stay long, may we go upstairs and put it in her room?"

"Please?" Bess begged. "My baby sister is lighter than this!"

"Well, okay, then!" Mrs. Tenowitz laughed,

stepping away from the door. "Sage's room is upstairs. It's the one with the stuffed animals on the bed."

The girls traded excited looks. Fishing? Stuffed animals? Double score!

Nancy, Bess, and George hurried upstairs. There they found a closed door with a sign: SAGE'S ROOM.

"Remember," Nancy said, opening the door, "we're only looking for a stuffed squirrel. That shouldn't be hard."

But when they stepped into Sage's room and looked around—

"Cheese and crackers!" George exclaimed.

Nancy's mouth dropped open. All around Sage's room were piles and piles of stuffed animals—on her bed! On her shelves! Even across her windowsill!

"There are more animals in here than the Bronx Zoo!" George groaned.

"Hundreds!" Bess confirmed as she placed the pumpkin on the floor. "Finding a stuffed squirrel in here will be like finding an eyelash in a sand castle!"

"I know! I know," Nancy agreed. "But we can't give up!"

Nancy's eyes darted around Sage's room. They suddenly landed on something in the corner. It wasn't another stuffed animal—it was a pink fishing pole!

"That's got to be the fishing pole from the video!" Nancy said, pointing at the corner. "Now all we have to do is find that squirrel."

George studied the animals on Sage's bed. "You know . . . there's something creepy about all these fake eyes watching us."

"Oh, don't be silly, George," Bess scoffed as she approached the bed. "How can this stuffed fluffy kitty be scary?"

Smiling, Bess reached out to touch the white cat when—

"MEEEEOOOWWWWW!!!"

Nancy, Bess, and George jumped back as a howling cat leaped from the stuffed-animal pile and off the bed.

"Omigosh!!!" Bess cried. "It's alive! It's alive!"

Chapter

7

CREEPY CAPE-R

The howling cat scooted under the bed when—

Tap-tap, tap-tap, tap-tap, tap-tap!

"What's that?" Nancy whispered. She, Bess, and George whirled around. Sage was walking toward them wearing tap shoes. The tapping stopped as Sage stepped on the carpet.

"My mom said you were up here." Sage scrunched her brow in confusion. "What are you doing?"

Nancy pointed down at the painted pumpkin. "We came to give you that."

Sage raised an eyebrow.

"And to look for a stuffed squirrel we saw swinging from a fishing pole in the parade," George admitted. "Do you know where we can find one?"

"Wh-why are you looking for it in my room?" Sage stammered.

"See for yourself," George said. She took out her tablet and then ran the recording, holding it up for Sage to see.

"Deirdre wanted Pom-Pom to lead the Howl-a-ween Parade more than any of the dogs," Nancy explained. "You said you would do anything for Deirdre so you could hang out with her."

"Like maybe make Chip bark at a stuffed squirrel on a fishing pole," Bess added. She pointed to the corner. "A pink fishing pole!"

Sage gulped loudly. "So I have a pink fishing pole, but I don't have a stuffed squirrel."

Nancy saw Sage's eyes dart to an open backpack on her desk. Sticking out of it was a bushy gray tail!

"What's in the bag, Sage?" Nancy asked.

"Not a stuffed squirrel!" Sage insisted. As she reached for the backpack, it toppled off the chair. It hit the floor with a *PLUNK* and out spilled—

"Squirrel!" George declared. "Bushy tail and all!"

"It's not the same squirrel from the parade!" Sage insisted. "Honest!"

George pointed to the fishing pole. "Then how do you explain the gray fuzz stuck on the fishing hook? Hmmm?"

"Um . . ." Sage hesitated. "Because some fish grow fur when it gets cold?"

"Stop being so squirrelly, Sage," George urged, "and tell us what really happened."

"Please?" Bess asked.

Sighing, Sage squeezed between a giant stuffed gorilla and giraffe to sit on her bed. Her shoulders dropped as she began to explain. "Deirdre did ask me to wave the stuffed squirrel in front of the wagon, so I did, but that's not what made Chip act weird."

"What do you mean?" Nancy asked.

"Chip was already acting weird before I waved the squirrel," Sage insisted. "I saw it myself, so it wasn't my fault!"

Nancy wondered if Sage was telling the truth. Did something else make Chip act weird? There had to be a way to find out.

"Could you play the video of the parade again, George?" Nancy asked.

"As soon as I turn the sound back on," George answered. "I forgot to turn it on after we left the park."

The girls huddled around George's tablet as they watched the parade, this time with sound.

Sage's squirrel had not yet appeared, but in the background, Chip's barks and whines were loud and clear!

"Hear that?" Sage said. "Deirdre thought my squirrel did the trick, but I know it didn't."

"Why didn't you tell Deirdre?" Bess asked.

"I wanted Deirdre to think I did a good job." Sage sighed. "So she'd let me hang out with her and her friends."

Nancy felt bad for Sage. She didn't seem excited about being friends with Deirdre. Not at all!

"Do you still want to be friends with Deirdre, Sage?" Nancy asked. "After you got to see what she's really like?"

"Not really," Sage admitted. "Deirdre acts totally snooty and bosses everyone around. I'd rather hang out with you guys!"

Nancy, Bess, and George smiled.

"You can hang with us anytime, Sage," Nancy said.

"Sure!" George agreed. "Thanks for getting real about the stuffed squirrel."

The Clue Crew said good-bye to Sage. As they headed away from the Tenowitz house, Nancy pulled out her Clue Book.

"Deirdre's plan didn't work on Chip," Nancy said, crossing her name off the list. "So Deirdre and Sage are innocent."

"I guess the stuffed squirrel's off the hook too," George joked. "The *fishing hook*—get it?"

"Ugh, George, please," Bess groaned.

Nancy put away her Clue Book. "Halloween is in two days, but I can't think about trick-or-treating. All I can think about is solving this mystery!"

"There's someone who's getting an early start on Halloween," George said, pointing up the block.

Nancy saw Quincy, dressed as a medieval knight, walking toward them. Clutched in one hand was an orange bag.

"Are you trick-or-treating already?" Nancy asked.

Quincy was about to speak when the visor of his plastic helmet fell over his face. He didn't seem to mind as he spoke through it. "One of the Ghost Grabbers had a Halloween party." Quincy's voice was muffled as he explained.

"Any ghosts show up?" George teased.

"No, but we would've known what to do if they did!" Quincy insisted before lifting his visor. "Have you decided to use Ghost Grabbers to find out what happened to Chip?"

Nancy shook her head. "We're solving this mystery on our own."

"And how is that working out for you?" Quincy grilled.

Nancy, Bess, and George remained silent. With Deirdre and Sage innocent, they had no more suspects.

"I thought so." Quincy chuckled before— CLUNK—the visor fell again.

"What a silly costume for a Halloween party," Bess whispered as Quincy walked away. "Bobbing for apples would be an epic fail!"

"What's really silly is what Quincy and his

Ghost Grabbers think," Nancy said. "As if Murray the Monster Mutt is a ghost who wants his old cape back!"

George reached deep into her backpack. "I just remembered something, Nancy. I picked up Chip's cape after it fell at the parade."

The Murray the Monster Mutt cape brought back sad memories of the parade for Nancy, but she thanked George as she took it.

"What next?" George asked. "Should we look for more clues on Main Street?

"Let's go home before it gets dark," Nancy suggested. "We can work on the case tomorrow."

"Tomorrow will be the day before Halloween!" Bess announced. "What are you wearing to go trick-or-treating on Monday?"

"If we don't solve this mystery tomorrow"— Nancy sighed—"I'll be wearing a frown!"

"Guess what show I ordered, Nancy?" Mr. Drew asked that evening after dinner.

Nancy's eyes brightened as she followed her dad

into the den. "Something spooky for Halloween?" she asked. "Not too spooky, I hope, Daddy!"

"More hokey than spooky." Mr. Drew chuckled. "It's the first three episodes of the *Murray the Monster Mutt Show*!"

"Awesome, Daddy. Thanks!" Nancy declared. Finally, she would see what the show was all about. And see the real Murray! Nancy sat in her favorite beanbag chair with Chocolate Chip at her feet.

"Hope it's a howl!" Mr. Drew joked after setting up the first show. He then left the den to help Hannah in the kitchen.

"It's showtime, Chip!" Nancy told her dog.

The opening credits filled the screen: "Murray the Monster Mutt starring as Murray the Monster Mutt." The first scene showed a girl walking a tiny white poodle. Suddenly, she hears a loud *"Woooooo!"* Frantic, the girl picks up her dog and begins to run. Looking over her shoulder, the girl sees who's chasing her. It's Murray the Monster Mutt—his famous cape flapping in the night breeze!

"Daddy was right, Chip." Nancy giggled. "This show isn't scary at all."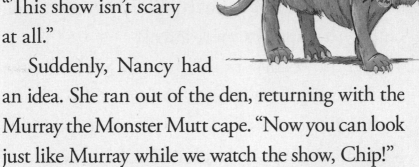

Suddenly, Nancy had an idea. She ran out of the den, returning with the Murray the Monster Mutt cape. "Now you can look just like Murray while we watch the show, Chip!"

Nancy tied the cape around Chip's neck. Chip's tail wagged cheerily, but a few seconds later—"*Woof, woof, whine, whine!*"

Surprised, Nancy stepped back as Chip barked, whined, and rolled just like she did on the hay wagon!

"*Woof, woof!*" Roll, kick. "*Whine, whine!*" Roll, kick. "*Woof!*" Roll. "*Whine!*" Kick. "*Woooooooo!!!*"

"Chip, you're acting like a Monster Mutt!" Nancy declared. Monster? Nancy looked at Chip and then at Murray on the TV.

"Omigosh—could Quincy be right?" Nancy wondered. "Could Chip's cape be haunted by Murray the Monster Mutt?"

Nancy decided to do a little experiment. She caught Chip and untied the cape. After taking away the cape, she watched Chip. It wasn't long before her puppy calmed down!

"Hmm," Nancy said to herself. She wrote the results in her Clue Book: *Cape off = Chip calm!*

But Nancy wasn't done with the experiment yet. She tied the cape around Chip's neck and then stepped back. After a few seconds—

"Woof, woof!" Roll, kick. *"Whine, whine!"* Roll, kick. *"Woof!"* Roll. *"Whine!"* Kick. *"Woooooooo!!!"*

Nancy's heart did a triple flip as she wrote the latest results in her Clue Book: *Cape on = Chip nuts!*

She glanced up from her Clue Book. Chip was now rolling around and around on the rug like a dog possessed!

"Maybe Quincy was right," Nancy said slowly. "Maybe the ghost of Murray the Monster Mutt does want his cape back!"

Chapter

8

TRICK OR RETREAT

"Do we have to go inside that creepy-looking house?" Bess gulped.

Nancy nodded her head slowly. It was Sunday morning, the morning after her cape-on, cape-off experiment. The results made her add Murray the Ghost-Dog to her suspect list!

"I called Quincy last night," Nancy explained. "He told me we should meet him at this house on Whisper Street where Murray used to live."

"When he was alive." Bess shuddered. "And maybe after."

The girls stared at the peeling paint on the house, a broken window, and what looked like cobwebs hanging from the porch.

"So what are we going to do in there?" George asked.

"Quincy told me we'll look for Murray's ghost," Nancy explained. "When we find him, we'll give him this!"

Nancy held up the vampire cape she had brought along. George's dark curls bounced as she shook her head.

"Can't you see Quincy is playing with us?" George asked. "He wants you to think Chip's cape is haunted so we'd call Ghost Grabbers!"

Nancy stuffed the cape inside her jacket pocket as Quincy and his Ghost Grabber friends headed toward them. All four kids wore matching sweats. In their hands were flashlights, badminton rackets, and a camera.

"Meet Liam, Kendall, and Tabitha," Quincy

introduced. "We knew you'd see things the Ghost Grabber way sooner or later."

"Did you bring the cape?" Kendall asked Nancy.

"Got it," Nancy said, nodding down at her pocket.

"Good," Quincy said. "Then it's all systems go!"

"Not so fast!" George warned. "Nancy isn't totally sure Chip's cape is haunted by Murray, right, Nancy?"

"Right," Nancy admitted. "I'm not sure I believe in ghosts."

"Ha!" Kendall laughed.

"That's what they all say!" Liam snorted.

Bess stepped forward. "If we're going to go inside that creepy place, can we please get it over with?"

"Okay," Quincy replied, "but first the Ghost Grabber rules: If you see a ghost, no screaming. And leave the grabbing to us. Any questions?"

"Just one," Nancy said. "How can you grab a ghost? Wouldn't your hands go right through?"

Quincy exchanged puzzled looks with his friends. He then turned to Nancy and said, "Too many questions. Let's get to work!"

The Clue Crew and Ghost Grabbers stepped up on the old wooden porch.

"What if it's locked?" Nancy asked.

"You're kidding me, right?" Quincy chuckled. "Haunted houses are always abandoned."

"Except for the ghosts!" Liam added.

Quincy grabbed the rusted old door handle and gave it a twist. The door opened with a creak.

"Whoa," George murmured as they filed inside the house.

Not only was it dark, there were cobwebs draped over the staircase banister, and creepy framed portraits were on the walls. This definitely looked like a haunted house!

Nancy pointed to a portrait of a dog wearing a dark cape. "That's Murray!"

"When he was alive," Liam said. Then he laughed, "Mwah, hah, hah."

"Are you sure that *portrait* isn't alive?" Bess gulped. "The eyes are moving back and forth as if they're watching us!"

Nancy noticed it too. She also noticed two doggy dishes on the floor against the wall. One was filled with water, and the other was filled with dog food.

"Ghosts don't eat," Nancy pointed out. "And if Murray was alive years ago why would his food be fresh?"

"The water would have evaporated too," Bess agreed. "We learned that in school."

George pointed to the floor. "Check out those muddy paw prints. They look pretty fresh too."

"Ghosts don't have feet," Bess shared. "Do they, Quincy?"

"Too many questions!" Quincy exclaimed. "Are we going to look through this house for Murray's ghost or what?"

"Wait!" George said. She began sniffing the air. "What's that smell?"

"Liam's sneakers?" Tabitha asked.

"No!" George sniffed again. "It suddenly smells in here like rotting leaves. Or rotting . . . something else."

"I smell it too," Nancy agreed, taking a whiff. "It didn't smell like this when we came in!"

"Where's it coming from?" Bess asked.

For the first time, the Ghost Grabbers looked worried too. Quincy opened his mouth to speak when—*"Wooooooo!!!"*

"What was that?" Quincy yelped.

Kendall's eyes popped wide open. "It—it—it sounds like—"

"Murray the Monster Mutt!" Liam cried.

Quincy turned to Nancy, Bess, and George, his face beaded with sweat. "Um . . . I just remembered I have a soccer game right now!"

"I have math tutoring!" Kendall added.

"Karate!" Tabitha uttered.

"Cake decorating!" Liam squeaked.

The Clue Crew watched as the Ghost Grabbers charged out the door.

"Should we leave too?" Bess asked.

Nancy wanted to leave but was curious about the strange sounds and smells. She was about to answer when—

"Getting a head start on your trick-or-treating?" someone with a deep voice asked from behind them.

The girls whirled around and froze. Stepping out from the shadows was a tall man dressed in black. His bushy eyebrows matched the shock of white hair on his head.

Nancy gulped at the sight of the creepy guy inside the creepy house. "Who's he?" Nancy whispered.

"Maybe Murray is more than a ghost-dog," George exclaimed. "Maybe he's a shape-shifter, too!"

Chapter

SOUR POWER

A small smile spread across the man's face. "Oh, I assure you. Murray is neither a ghost nor a shape-shifter."

"How do you know?" George asked.

"I'm Max, Murray's owner and manager," Max replied. "I knew Murray very well . . . and still do!"

"Still do?" Bess asked. "You mean . . . ?"

Max stuck two fingers in his mouth and whistled. After a few seconds, a grizzled old dog padded into the entrance hall next to Max. The girls stared at the old dog. Could it be what they thought it was?

"Is that Murray?" Nancy asked.

"He's alive!" George exclaimed.

Max stooped to scratch Murray's fuzzy hunched back. "Murray is very much alive." He laughed. "He doesn't get out much anymore, just for short walks three times a day."

"But Murray used to be a star!" Nancy said. "I saw his show myself!"

"Murray is too old to act on television," Max said. "Instead, he likes to snooze by the fire or watch old tapes of his show." Max smiled proudly at his dog. "But he still howls the same way he used to!"

"We know!" Bess giggled covering her ears.

"If Murray isn't a ghost," George said, looking around, "why does this place look like a haunted house?"

Max heaved a big, sad sigh. "Every year I decorate this old house for Halloween," Max explained.

"I even keep the door unlocked days before Halloween in case I get visitors." Max shook his head and said, "But hardly any kids come trick-or-treating because they think it's really haunted."

"We thought so too, Max," Nancy admitted. "The portrait with the moving eyes gave us goose bumps."

"So did that icky, rotten smell that came out of nowhere!" Bess added. "P. U!"

Max looked happy to explain: "The portrait with the moving eyes was a prop in the *Murray the Monster Mutt Show*. As for the smell, it comes from a special aromatherapy machine I bought for Murray."

"Aromatherapy?" Nancy repeated. "Like a smell machine?"

"This one is called A-Rover-Therapy." Max nodded. "It fills the room with smells dogs love and people don't. Like rotten meat, sweaty sneakers—"

"Gross smells," Bess cut in. She wrinkled her nose. "We get it."

"There it is." Max pointed to a small table in the hall. On it was a black box with a round dial on the top.

"Sweet!" George declared. "I want to check it out!"

As George headed toward the A-Rover-Therapy machine, Max called, "Stop!"

George froze in her tracks. "Why? I just want to check out the new gadget."

"You might accidentally turn the dial to citrus fruits," Max said, "and dogs hate the smell of citrus fruits!"

"Then why is it on the machine?" Nancy asked.

"It's for when owners want to keep dogs out of a room," Max explained. "Like when they're setting up for a party. Or if there's a newborn baby."

Max gave the girls permission to pet Murray. The retired pet celeb seemed to like the attention as his gray-streaked tail waved back and forth.

"We'd better go now," Nancy said, "but we're

going to tell our friends to come trick-or-treating here tomorrow!"

"And meet Murray the Monster Mutt!" Bess declared. "A real superstar!"

"That would be wonderful!" Max boomed. "Don't leave without Murray's pawtograph!"

A pawtograph was an autograph with a paw print instead of a signature. Max handed Murray's pawtographs to Nancy, Bess, and George!

The girls thanked Max and Murray, but as they walked under Murray's portrait toward the door Nancy remembered something. . . .

"I have Murray's old vampire cape, Max," Nancy said. "Would you and Murray like it back?"

"Keep the cape as a memento!" Max declared. "A memento of Murray the Monster Mutt!"

"Woof," Murray barked weakly.

Outside, Nancy crossed Murray the Ghost-Dog from her suspect list.

"I'm glad Murray isn't a ghost," Bess said.

Nancy glanced back at the old house. Murray

wasn't a ghost, but it still didn't explain everything.

"If Murray isn't a ghost," Nancy wondered out loud, "then why does Chip go nutty each time she wears the cape?"

"I don't know," Bess admitted, "but at least we got to meet Murray."

"I wish I could have checked out that smell machine," George said. "What are citrus fruits anyway?"

"Don't you remember from school, George?" Bess asked. "Some citrus fruits are lemons, limes, and oranges."

Lemons? The word caused Nancy's heart to skip a beat. She stopped walking to stare at Bess and George.

"What's up, Nancy?" George asked.

"You look like you just saw a ghost," Bess said. "Which would be crazy because we know Murray isn't one!"

"I didn't see a ghost," Nancy insisted, "but I did remember something—something important!"

Clue Crew—and YOU!

Ready to think like the Clue Crew and solve what happened to Chocolate Chip? It's your turn to get a piece of paper and crack this case—or turn the page to find out!

1. The Clue Crew ruled out Felipe Gomez, Deirdre, plus the ghost of Murray the Monster Mutt. Who else could have wanted Chip out of the parade? List your suspects on a sheet of paper.

2. When Nancy heard "lemon" she remembered something superimportant. Why would lemons be a clue, and why would they upset Chip? Write down your answers on a sheet of paper.

3. Nancy likes writing her suspects and clues in a Clue Book. If you were a detective, what tools would you use? Make your list on a sheet of paper.

Chapter

THE NOSE KNOWS

"What did we use to wash Chip's cape to get the skunk stink out?" Nancy asked.

Bess scrunched her brow trying to remember their special concoction. "I know we used tomato juice," Bess recalled. "And vinegar—"

"And lemons!" George cut in. "Lots of lemon juice!"

"Bingo!" Nancy exclaimed. "Max said dogs hate the smell of citrus fruit. Maybe a lemony smell stayed on the cape after I rinsed it!"

Bess tapped her chin thoughtfully. "Which could have made Chip nutty every time she wore it!" Bess said slowly before her eyes lit up. "That's got to be it!"

"Or not!" George disagreed. "What if Max made that up to keep me from touching the smell machine?"

Nancy thought George had a point, but there was a way to find out. "Do a search on your tablet, George," Nancy urged, "for smells dogs hate."

Nancy and Bess peered over George's shoulders as she typed in the question. The first thing that popped up was a clip from Felipe's webisode *The Peaceful Pet*!

"Felipe Gomez!" Bess pointed to the screen. "What a coincidence!"

"Let's see what he talks about," Nancy said.

George pressed the arrow to start the video. It showed a smiling Felipe who said, "Want to know how to keep your dog from jumping on the sofa? Try the Felipe Way and spray your sofa with lemon juice!"

The girls watched Felipe use a spray bottle to squirt a sofa. A Maltese pup lazing on the sofa perked up. With a whine, he immediately hopped off.

"If lemon juice doesn't work, try vinegar, another smell dogs hate," Felipe suggested. "It's not just for salads anymore!"

Nancy, Bess, and George traded excited looks.

"You washed Chip's cape in lemon *and* vinegar!" Bess told Nancy.

"But if the skunk smell came out in the wash," George wondered, "why not the lemon and vinegar smell?"

Nancy didn't really know. But she did have an idea . . . "Let's go to my house," Nancy suggested. "It's time for another experiment."

Nancy held up the lemon slice her dad had cut for them before going out to rake leaves. "One lemon slice!"

"One lemon slice," Bess repeated. "Check!"

The Clue Crew stood huddled around the

Drews' kitchen table. On it was Nancy's Clue Book opened to the experiments page. Also on the table were ingredients for Nancy's experiment.

"We can't do the experiment without Chip." Nancy called her puppy into the kitchen.

Chip scurried in happily, wagging her tail.

"Chip thinks she's getting a treat," Bess whispered.

"She will," Nancy promised. "But first . . ."

Nancy stuck the lemon slice beneath Chip's nose. Chip sniffed. She let out a snort and backed away!

"Chip doesn't like the smell!" George declared.

Nancy wrote the first result in her Clue Book: *Lemon Slice = Retreat!*

"Next step," Nancy announced as she reached for a bottle of vinegar. The moment she removed the cap the sour scent filled the kitchen. With a whine, Chip darted out of the room!

"Chip *really* hated that one!" George remarked.

Bess squeezed her nose. "She's not the only one!"

Nancy beamed as she wrote the result in her Clue Book: *Vinegar = Bolt!*

Next in her Clue Book, Nancy wrote: *Culprits = Lemon juice and vinegar. Case closed!*

"Experiment a success!" Nancy stated.

The Clue Crew high-fived. They then found Chip in the den to give her a well-deserved treat.

"I'm glad we figured out what upset Chip," Bess said as Chip crunched on a biscuit. "It's just too bad she never got to lead the Howl-a-ween Parade."

"Yeah," George agreed. "She would have been an awesome mutt-ster of ceremonies!"

Chip glanced up from her biscuit. Her ears wiggled as she cocked her head.

"Don't worry, Chip," Nancy said with a smile. "Howl-a-ween may have been a bummer—but there's still Halloween!"

And Nancy had a plan!

"Check out all the kids smiling at Chip!" Bess pointed out the next day.

"I know!" Nancy said excitedly. "It's like Chip is a canine celebrity!"

It was after school on Halloween and time for some serious trick-or-treating. Chip was dressed head to tail but not as Murray the Monster Mutt. Today she was dressed as another TV dog with a cape: Detective Sherlock Hound. After all, Chip did have a nose for solving mysteries!

"Are you sure they're smiling at Chip," George muttered as they walked down a street filled with other trick-or-treaters, "or are they laughing at our superweird costumes?"

Bess's pointy blue crayon cap wobbled as she shook her head. All three friends were dressed up as crayons—red, yellow, and blue.

"Our costumes rock, George!" Bess said. "But Chip is the star of trick-or-treat!"

"And if anyone knows about treats," George joked, "it's Chip!"

"Totally!" Nancy agreed with a big smile. "And if anyone knows about solving mysteries, it's the Clue Crew!"

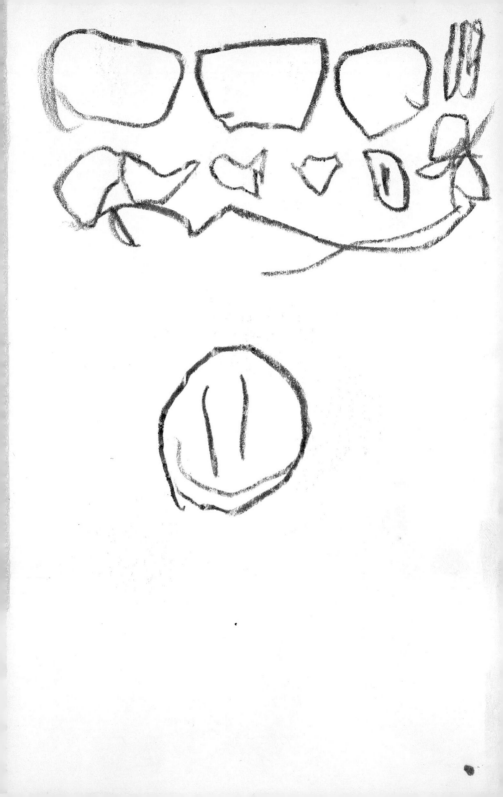